Daughter of a Brazilian mother and Portuguese father, Valentina Agnes was born in Brazil. Since her childhood, she has shown a lot of ability to turn small facts into big stories, through her original and creative way of telling stories full of mystery and entertainment. But it was at the age of 12 years old, in 2017, that Valentina really decided to write down her ideas, turning them into stories of adventure and mystery.

For my mom, Fernanda, thank you for the support.

Valentina Agnes

THE LAST ONES

Copyright © Valentina Agnes 2023

All rights reserved. No part of this publication may be reproduced, distributed, or transmitted in any form or by any means, including photocopying, recording, or other electronic or mechanical methods, without the prior written permission of the publisher, except in the case of brief quotations embodied in critical reviews and certain other non-commercial uses permitted by copyright law. For permission requests, write to the publisher.

Any person who commits any unauthorized act in relation to this publication may be liable to criminal prosecution and civil claims for damages.

This is a work of fiction. Names, characters, businesses, places, events, locales, and incidents are either the products of the author's imagination or used in a fictitious manner. Any resemblance to actual persons, living or dead, or actual events is purely coincidental.

Ordering Information
Quantity sales: Special discounts are available on quantity purchases by corporations, associations, and others. For details, contact the publisher at the address below.

Publisher's Cataloging-in-Publication data
Agnes, Valentina
The Last Ones

ISBN 9798886937077 (Paperback)
ISBN 9798886937084 (Hardback)
ISBN 9798886937091 (Audiobook)
ISBN 9798886937107 (ePub e-book)

Library of Congress Control Number: 2023906372

www.austinmacauley.com/us

First Published 2023
Austin Macauley Publishers LLC
40 Wall Street, 33rd Floor, Suite 3302
New York, NY 10005
USA

mail-usa@austinmacauley.com
+1 (646) 5125767

I would like to thank the wonderful teachers at George C. Marshall High School who have been by my side, encouraging me to do my best as a student. It was the generous and wise words of these professionals that encouraged me to evolve as a reader and writer. And I also want to thank my mother who never allowed obstacles to become barriers in the pursuit of my goals. I thank my mother who showed me the importance of fighting to make my dreams come true. A respectful and loving to thank you to all of you.

Table of Contents

Preface	**11**
Chapter 1: The Chosen Ones	**12**
Chapter 2: The Mansion	**19**
Chapter 3: Two Sharp Points	**30**
Chapter 4: The Curse	**38**
Chapter 5: On the Other Side of the Mountain	**44**
Chapter 6: The Discovery	**52**
Chapter 7: Competing in the Dark	**60**
Chapter 8: The Ally	**65**
Chapter 9: The Big Day	**73**

Preface

Many families hide great mysteries and sacrifices to achieve a position of status in society. Anything to stay on top is acceptable. Among them, agreements with entities of nature, where the price of the contract is worth a life. A curse that can only be lifted if the soul shows that it deserves to live. How to defend your life in the face of a curse? What makes someone earn the right to live?

Chapter 1
The Chosen Ones

I always liked this teacher, Ms. Smith. I took several history classes with her during my high school and my grades were always A. Partly because I like history a million times more than math, but also because Ms. Smith has always been very generous to me. She felt sorry because she realized that I was bullied for being the daughter of Venezuelans and felt that other kids always got more attention than I did. The truth is that I was a baby when my parents left Venezuela in search of a safer life in the United States, so my memories do not bring back anything from my home country. I grew up in Northern Virginia and never visited Venezuela, in fact, my family lost a lot of money when they left Venezuela, so we were never able to go on long trips, my parents had to work extremely hard so that we could go on with our life here and never have to return to that place ruled by corrupt and inhumane politicians. Class was particularly interesting today. Ms. Smith told the story of a curse that had happened in the exact year I was born. She said it was the legend of worthless children. It was the story of couples who could not get pregnant and looked for an indigenous entity to be blessed, but along with the miraculous blessing of the fertile uterus came a curse where each baby at the age of 18 would be tested to see if the most important moral values had been reasserted to that kid who was blessed in his conception. If the parents who wanted so much to have a child had not passed on the values that make a human being worthy of a miracle to exist, the family and the kid would suffer physical consequences equivalent to spiritual deficiencies. At the same time, I looked at girl sitting near me, and wished she were one of those children of the legend, that something bad would happen to her, because she was so snobby that even the teachers could not tolerate such arrogance. There were so many students like her and with that same attitude that I could not take it anymore. My group of friends was non-existent. I had some peers that I interacted with on some tasks and at the Spanish club where I was president. I will not even mention my love life, it would be a disaster to remember that the only time I fell in love with a boy and wrote him a letter declaring myself, I had to stay at home for a week with the excuse that I was sick, but actually I was ashamed of myself. Walking in the school hallways after everyone has seen my romantic letter, that idiot boy has decided to share on his Instagram. Now everybody knows. Oh my god I hate that boy. From that moment on, if I find someone interesting, I keep quiet. It is also a lot of work trying to look pretty for others. My skin is covered in pimples, and I do not know what else to do to improve it other than using makeup that my mother taught me how to use. There is no cream that can make this hell out of my face. My thoughts were interrupted by the signal. It was time to go home and continue my senior year countdown. It was not long before I graduated high school with honors and finally this school and these silly teenagers. When I got home, I noticed that my mother was nervous and distressed holding a letter in her hand while arguing with my father. I could not hear what they were arguing about because as soon as I walked into the room they stopped talking. My head swiveled 360 degrees because immediately I knew something was serious and it was about me. At that moment, they tried to disguise the tension that was in the environment and said we would talk later after all my father was doing a construction budget for an important businessperson and he could not explain at that moment what was happening. Well, I did not pay much attention to all that nervousness either and went to my room. My room was my universe, mine alone. I was an only child, so I had all the privacy I needed to watch TV and follow beautiful boys on social media. Sometimes one or the other even followed me back or started a conversation with me, but nothing concrete. I even tried to post beautiful photos full of filter and editing, but I did not feel beautiful like that, in fact, I even tried to cover and hide my face letting my hair fall on top. It was hard for me to feel beautiful, and I wanted it so much. I wanted to be so that some guy would come after me. I was tall, thin, I had light tanned skin, had long blonde hair and light green eyes, but it was all hidden behind that bunch of pimples and glasses on my face. Eventually I fell asleep and woke up to my mother knocking on my bedroom door and calling me to dinner. When gathered around the table, my father came calmly to initiate the subject of the letter they had received.

"My daughter, we have received an invitation to a competition for a scholarship for you and we need you to participate, in fact your presence has already been confirmed," said my father. There was a pause for my brain to understand what he was talking about until my mother said: "It's just a competition but we need you to represent our family." I was even more intrigued. Competition? Scholarship? Represent family? Completely lost, I asked the details of this championship because I did not even practice sports, I had no talent to compete in any modality for sure. My father replied saying that in this competition other talents would be tested and that he did not know more details, only that I should go and that would happen during Spring Break vacation week. After I heard that I was going to lose my vacation in a competition I was being forced to go to, I did not even want to talk to my parents anymore. I was indignant at that absurdity, so I finished my dinner and rested in my room. The next day I found a letter with my name in bold, Camila Vergas, in the kitchen. I open the letter quickly and start reading what's inside.

Ladies and gentlemen,

Congratulations! If you have received this letter, you have been selected from among all high school students in Northern Virginia to be one of six who will enter the competition to win a scholarship. All six participants are senior year students who have recently turned 18. Participants in this competition, or rather this exclusive program, declare that they will not say anything about their participation to anyone other than their parents. The competition will be held at a place designated for such an event, where participants will reside for 5 consecutive days. During these 5 days there will be no contact with the outside world, only with the participants themselves. As for the contest rules, these will be delivered throughout the day during the competition, just stay alert.

As a prize, the winner will receive a full scholarship to study at any university in the United States.

Therefore, your presence will be expected on April 2nd, at 8am on Peyton Street, opposite West Park. Be punctual and remember that you can only bring a backpack with your essential personal items, nothing else.

See you soon!

Sincerely,
Mister X

I still could not believe that whole competition thing, it did not make any sense to me. On top of that, there was only a week to go until April 2nd. But it was better not to spend any more time trying to find out more about the competition that still had a geometry test this week and other papers to turn in. Lucky for this Mister X, who asked to keep this as a secret, I don't have any friends at school because it would be hard not to tell. "But had someone else from my school been called? Only 6 students competed, what a small number," thoughts running my mind.

The week flew by as doubts about such a competition flew in my imagination. The big day was already tomorrow, and I hadn't even made the backpack to take with me. I didn't even know what to bring, I had no idea what I would need, but I remember that in the letter it was clear that I could only take the essentials. Already nervous for the day that would come tomorrow I tried to pack my backpack with my survival items like clothes and makeup, and of course my cell phone charger.

I woke up at 6 am to have time to wash my hair and get ready. That initial anger at the competition was over, I even liked the idea of going somewhere nice and meeting other students. The idea of vacations also appealed me even though I knew I would have to participate in some activities. I got dressed and chose the clothes I thought were perfect for my body: jeans that made me look toned, and a beautiful sweater I had bought with my mother last Christmas. I thought about wearing boots with little heels, but I opted for comfortable sneakers after all in case I needed to run or something similar. That backpack didn't have room for shoes, so those shoes were the only ones I'd have in the house during the competition. I took my last look in the mirror and went to the kitchen where my parents were waiting to take me to the designated meeting place for the participants.

My father, a wise and hardworking man, told me: "Don't miss any opportunity to show your best. Show the wonderful person that you are." While my mother filled me with kisses and hugs whispering with tears in her eyes saying: "We love you my daughter, good luck!" And it was in this funereal atmosphere that I left home. In just a few minutes, we arrived at the place, and I finally said goodbye to my parents.

The first thing I saw when I got out of the car was a black bus with all the windows covered parked in front of the park. Immediately, I saw that a very beautiful athletic woman was screaming my name. I walked towards her until she introduced herself, saying that her name was Barbara, and that she would be our instructor during the competition. Without further formality, Barbara handed me a tag with my name, and told me to always have the tag in sight. Then, still smiling, she spoke the first order of the competition: "Well Camila, now you're going to get on the bus, sit in the place you want sit without getting in touch with any of the other participants until you're told otherwise." Those words fell like an ice bucket on my head, how cold and harsh that woman was. My excitement was all gone, I just wanted to go back to my room.

As soon as I got on the bus, I noticed that all the other students were already there. Then the instructor Brabara got in and before the bus driver could start, she gave the following message:

"Good morning, everyone, welcome. I will be the person who will guide you to the place of the competition. However, so we can start I want to collect all your cell phones, but don't worry that no one will touch them, and you will have him back as soon as the championship is over."

My world is definitely over. Hell has begun.

Chapter 2
The Mansion

In less than 1 hour, in total silence during the journey, we arrived in front of this old mansion. It looked like an abandoned house in the middle of a very thick forest. It had 2 floors and a balcony that ran along the entire front of the house. It was then that Barbara asked us all to get off the bus and she would do the honors of the house and explain the next steps.

When I entered the house, I was even amazed because looking from the outside it looked much worse than the inside. The house was warm and pleasant, which relieved me as it was still quite cold in northern Virginia in early April. The house had a large living room with leather sofas in front of a huge fireplace, as well as other antique furniture, including a long wooden table and a very spacious kitchen.

As I looked around the house I was interrupted by Barbara:

"I want everyone's attention, please. This will be your home for the next few days. Each of you will have your own room which is identified with the respective names on the door and are located on the upper floor. No one will be in this house but you. If you pay attention, you will see that there is a Sound Box installed in all the rooms of the house, so I suggest that you pay attention to it because it will be through it that you will be called to take the tests and receive other instructions. I suggest that now you take the opportunity to talk, and get to know each other better since you haven't done so yet, and take the opportunity to go up to your respective rooms. There you will also find bath towels and numbered clothes that will be used during the Championship. As you arrived today, lunch is already prepared in advance in the kitchen. You will have pizza and just need heat it up. Any questions?" said Barbara in a serious and harsh tone.

At this point, Emily asked:

"Hi, and how are we going to make the other meals?"

Barbara said we'd find out all about that later. After such a rude answer, no one wanted to ask any more questions. Barbara then left the house and closed the door.

As soon as she left we all looked at each other and finally started talking. It was a mixture of feelings because nobody was understanding this competition. We spread out across the room and started talking to each other. And it was a relief to realize that it wasn't just me who was afflicted.

We were 3 girls; Emily, Grace, and I and 3 more boys; Daniel, Thomas, and John. No one was from my school, but there was a boy, handsome by the way, Daniel, who I had seen him before, because he played hockey precisely with that boy, that in the past I was in love with, and delivered the blessed letter. My hope at that time was that he wouldn't bully me about the letter, in fact it would have been better if he had never heard of me. With the way he was handsome, and seemed to come from a wealthy family, he was much more likely to look at Emily than me. Emily looked like a version of a doll she was so well made. Blonde, doll-faced with full lips, a slim waist, and full curves. She was beautiful and, above all, she seemed very friendly and extroverted, that is, it was impossible not to be jealous of that girl. I also spoke with Grace, who was more introverted, but we quickly talked about the distress of the trip inside of the bus where we could not see the road and now we had no idea where we were. Soon afterwards I also talked with Thomas and John. Daniel joined us and suggested that we all go up to the second floor to see the rooms and competition outfits.

The rooms really were all identified with the name of the participants on the door, and we also saw the 2 bathrooms, one for the girls and one for the boys. Inside each of the rooms we find the competition clothes identified by numbers. What I found strange was a diving suit after all it was winter and even if the suit was waterproof it would be tortured to go into a river or pool at that time. I noticed the sound box in the upper corner of my room and saw the red light on. I was intrigued if that wasn't also a camera recording my every move. Disturbing thoughts haunted my head. Initially, it was good to meet everyone, but those rooms without a television and with the windows covered so that no light could get in, started to make me tense. In a few minutes, I heard voices coming from the hall and I joining them, returning to the room along with the rest of the group. Soon we were all talking trying to imagine what would be the first test on the competition. Some thought it was a sport, others suggested it might be something to do with cognitive tests, others said it would be marathon workouts with all the high school content. Each one made their bet, but no one imagined what was to come.

Until John, pointing at the clock on the living room wall, said that we could have lunch, after all it was lunch time and in a joking tone he said that at his house, in the countryside, lunch was served very early. We all agreed and together we went to explore the kitchen this time. It had all the necessary utensils for cooking as well as a normal oven and microwave to everyone's delight, but it had absolutely no supplies, not even a pot of old salt. At least, the pizzas were all there and they were what we ate at that moment sitting around the long wooden table. As we finished our pizza, we heard Mister X's voice through the sound box for the first time.

"Welcome participants! We hope that you all enjoyed the facilities and the welcome pizza lunch, but as you may have noticed, there is no food in the house and so that you can cook and prepare your dinner, the first test of the competition will be the food test. At 1:30 pm, I want everyone ready in the room wearing uniform number 1. Barbara will pick you up and, in addition to explaining the test details, she will monitor the competition. Good luck everyone and the loser will soon be here with me." The calm and husky voice stopped and the light of the Sound Box that was green turned red again.

We all got up from the table and dropped our plates and glasses into the kitchen while we wondered who this Mister X was and where he was. John and I had the initiative to clean up the kitchen by picking up the mess and organizing everything. All participants before the scheduled time were already ready in the room waiting for Barbara. Punctually, Barbara arrived. That athletic, strong figure, seemed to have come out of a sculpture, but with a sad, unhappy face. I realized that, with me her reaction seemed to be different, because whenever she looked at me it was as if she were trying to smile. "Well, maybe she liked me, not bad." I thought so.

So, Barbara made us all follow her towards the forest to a certain place under a huge tree, there was something that looked like a rectangular box the size of a coffin covered by a black cloth. There she explained the proof:

"Heads up! This test is perhaps the most important of all, because your nutrition depends on it. In this area limited by the ropes, you will have to look for the keys that will open the food cupboards in the pantry. You will need to find 6 keys on the ground: 5 keys will be used to open the pantry and the other key will be used to open one of your colleagues, who will be trapped in an acrylic box surrounded by rats while you will be in the woods. The test will last as long as it takes for all the keys to be found and your colleague will not be able to give up the test otherwise you won't have food until tomorrow. The trapped participant may still be released during the course of the test if the key to his Acrylic Box is found before the end of the test. I will give you 15 minutes to discuss and define who will be the participant who will be trapped."

At that moment, I no longer felt my heart, I was so desperate, the only thing I managed to say was to beg my colleagues that I would not have any conditions to stay in a Box with rats. If I were the chosen one, we would all starve for sure. Then Emily and Grace said the same as me. So, I heard everyone talking at the same time until Daniel took the front of everyone raising his arm and said:

"Guys, let's organize. So, the girls already said that they can't stay in the Box, so it's up to me, Thomas, or John to stay with the rats. Is anyone down for that? But you really have to hold on, because this area is big and it's going to take us a while to find the keys." Promptly John, my newest bosom friend, volunteered and said that on the farm where he grew up he was used to all kinds of animals, and that he would put up with it. I heard everyone breathing in relief after listening to John. And right after that Thomas told John that he could rest assured that he was going to do his best to find the key to the Box of Rats as quickly as possible. Thomas seemed to be just that kind of person: agile and competitive. Daniel again said: "Since we decided who will be trapped, we could divide the area that each one will look for the key, so we don't waste time looking twice in the same place." As we pointed to areas and identified who would go to each location, Barbara arrived.

"So," said Barbara, "who's going to get into the Rat Box?"

John took a step forward and we saw her remove the cloth from the front of the Box. It was a funerary casket made of acrylic with lots of rats inside. I couldn't believe what I was seeing, and my eyes filled with tears when I saw my friend John entering that Box. It was the worst image I could see. As soon as he got in and she closed the lock on the Box, Barbara shouted: "Start it!" That was far from being a nest hunt like we do at Easter time.

It didn't take long, and I heard Emily scream saying she had found a key. We all celebrated that moment as she ran to the casket in an attempt to believe that it was the right key, but it wasn't. We keep looking. After a while, we heard Thomas screaming from far away saying that he had found another key, and again we were filled with hope of seeing John out of the Box, but again it was still not the right key. After some time, it was Grace's turn to find a key that wasn't the coffin key either. I was just thinking about John, poor guy. We were all with a thousand adrenaline turning the earth upside down, until I heard Daniel call me. He was lifting a piece of tree trunk and he said he saw something metallic gleam, so he asked me to help. "I'm going to lift this trunk and you try to reach that metal thing over there, it can only be one of the keys," he said. To our delight it was a key so without even celebrating that moment I ran as fast as I could to the coffin. Finally, it was the key to saving John. I couldn't contain myself with so much joy and when I saw my friend outside the coffin, I gave him a strong hug. With a smile on his face, he extended his hand to me and said: "Look what I have found." It was a key that had been left inside the coffin. At this point, it only remained to find one more key and we would be free. Together with John, we headed in the opposite direction from where I had already looked. As he related the coffin experience, I could see that Grace was sitting on top of a rock doing nothing. That made me angry to the core, but at that moment I tried to ignore it and keep looking. Before know, we heard a scream on the other side of, was Daniel saying that he had found the last key. It was the best moment of the day! Barbara, who followed everything from the top of a wooden platform, carrying the loudspeaker gave the statement:

"Attention all participants: race closed. Come all here in the starting position."

In minutes, we were all there. Then Barbara asked for everyone's attention so that she could announce the winner and the eliminated. We all didn't understand who would be eliminated, because in fact everyone found a key, even John who was inside the coffin. Without giving time for many questions Barbara said that the winner of the test was the person who had released the prisoner, and the loser of the test was the person nominated by the winner. The loser would have dinner with everyone, and the next day would be out of the house.

My happiness as a winner lasted seconds. First, because I hadn't found the key, the title of winner was more Daniel's than mine, but he said that I was brave to stick my hand where there could have been an animal, so I gave myself the credit for the victory. But nominating someone to leave the competition did not please me at all, because I would be hated by everyone. At that moment, I would have preferred a thousand times that Daniel had won the race. But anyway, Barbara looked at me and asked for the name of the participant I wanted to eliminate. My will, after finding the key together with Daniel, was to send that beautiful girl away, Emily, but I saw that the person who wasn't helping with the test was Grace. So, I used this argument that grace was sitting on a rock in the middle of the competition to justify her elimination.

The race ended and we were all able to return to the old mansion.

We were all euphoric that the first test of the competition was over, and we could finally open the pantry cupboards and the fridge. The only one who was clearly huffing, and puffing was Grace. As soon as we arrived at the house she came to question me: "Camila, why me? Why didn't you choose someone else? I thought we had become friends." I was all embarrassed, but had to respond, while the others also turned their full attention to our conversation. Calmly, without the aggressiveness that she used, I said: "Look Grace, I was forced to choose someone, and that has nothing to do with being your friend. I ran out of options and at that time the only thing I remembered was seeing you sitting in the rock there while everyone else was going crazy trying to get John out of the rat cage." I can see her face turning slightly red. "But you could have chosen at least one of the boys," she replied. I didn't want to say any more about that subject, I just told her that I do apologize, and that unfortunately it was part of the game. Paying no further attention to that girl, I joined those heading to the kitchen to open the pantry.

According to Barbara's instructions, from that moment until the next day we were on our own. It would be our time to shower and then prepare dinner. Finally, it was my turn to take off those dirty mud clothes and take a shower. When I went down to the room, I felt like a different person: I was clean and calmer now after we had taken the test, in addition to feeling much more at ease with the other participants.

I saw that Grace was looking at me angrily, but there was nothing I could do, and I also knew that she was leaving the next day, so I wasn't even trying to talk to her anymore. We all got together in the kitchen to make our dinner, the only ones who didn't help at all were Emily and Thomas, but the rest of the group managed to prepare a beautiful meal. In fact, Emily and Thomas did not help at all inside the house, causing comments among the rest of the group.

Each one served their plate, and we all went to the wooden table. We couldn't stop talking about Barbara's cool monitoring of our test, and we all agreed that she had a sad and melancholy look. Then we started talking about who Mister X could be, and where he would be housed. At this moment, Grace said: "I'd rather stay here with you, I didn't want to be the first eliminated, I don't even know where I'm going." Daniel and John tried to calm her down by saying that it would probably be a very comfortable hotel, and that a day later one of us would be there with her. There was no need to be nervous, because at that point there were people who no longer wanted to be there. It was a relief to be eliminated from that competition.

We finished our dinner and went to snuggle in front of the fireplace. John my new best friend sat next to me, while I watched Daniel right in front of me. Everyone told a little about themselves and their lives, we even seemed like good old friends chatting away. One fact, however, caught everyone's attention: we were all only children. We raised the question if that would have been a requirement to enter the competition, but nobody had the answer. Before we fell asleep right there, we said goodbye and we all went to sleep, but without first hearing Thomas: "Stay tuned girls, maybe Mister X is watching you change clothes in your room?" I could have gone to sleep without those words. Of course, when I changed clothes in my room I tried to hide behind the closet door, because that red light could be a camera, but rationally it would be too much, totally inappropriate.

It had been a long and emotional day. That test we did, leave me looking forward to what's to come. I didn't expect this kind of competition, but I also didn't expect to find a boy as interesting as Daniel. He was the leader in our race, which was important at the time, but when it came to questioning my winning award, he gave me all the credit, it was so sweet of him. But it was time to sleep, my body was relaxing, so I could feel the effort my legs had made that afternoon. Even without my usual TV in the room, I managed to fall asleep.

Chapter 3
Two Sharp Points

I woke up not having the slightest idea of the time. It was so dark in my room, due to the blocking of the windows, that made it difficult to know. I heard a noise coming from the bathroom, so I thought it was time to get up, and find out how the second day of competition would go.

I got ready and went down to have my breakfast. Little by little, the other participants appeared in the kitchen after all it was still early, the sun had just started to appear.

To my delight, my new best friend, John, was already there offering me cereal and milk. So far, getting to know John and Daniel, had been the best part of the competition. I don't know if Daniel noticed me in the same way I noticed him, probably not. But John was simply the sweetest person in this world: loving, delicate, and very playful. It was good to know that I had made a friend like him, and that we would definitely remain friends after that competition.

Emily arrived in the kitchen, said good morning, and asked what we were going to do, and what was the day's activity, but still no one had any idea. Soon after, we saw Thomas and Daniel show up for breakfast too. At that moment everyone was there, except Grace, Emily spoke in a low tone: "You know Camila, last night, Grace didn't stop talking bad about you. She said that you chose her, because you are a spoiled envious person, and that you only want to get close to boys, because they can help you much more than the girls." I didn't react and saw that the other boys nodded in agreement, confirming what Emily had said about Grace. John immediately looked at me and said: "Don't even pay attention to Grace's words, because you weren't the only one who saw that she wasn't helping in the test, and you had the right to choose someone. So forget about it." I agreed with a half-fake smile, but it was uncomfortable knowing that others were talking bad about me behind my back, but anyway, it was better to do as John said, and forget about it, because Grace was already leaving anyway.

"Guys, has anyone seen Grace? What time are they going to pick her up?" I asked everyone. Looking at Emily I said: "Let's go upstairs and look for her?" We went upstairs and called for Grace, and no sign of her until we walked into her room, and saw that the bed was all messed up, and the closet with her things was empty. We were stunned, and hurried down the stairs to let them know what had happened.

"Guys, no sign of Grace nor her things. I think she already left." They were all perplexed wondering what time she would have gone, and how nobody heard any noise. Daniel said: "Yesterday she said she didn't want to be the first to go to the other house or hotel or whatever, and she was hating it all. Did she not run away?" Thomas said, "For Grace to run away from here would be impossible. First, it was dark, and second, where would she go? Not one of us knows where we are. The road goes in 2 directions, and we can only see a tunnel of trees. I don't think she would risk leaving here in the middle of the night alone." And John said: "So, if Grace is not here anymore is, because Barbara must have come to get her before we woke up, during the night maybe." Better that way, was what I thought at the time. I'd rather know she was already somewhere safe than think she could have run off alone, and this was all my fault. What a hell of a competition, we didn't even have a phone to call, and find out what was going on. We stood there not knowing what to do until the green light on the speaker came on. "Attention all participants. I hope you had a wonderful night. During the morning, you can stay in the house. In the afternoon, you will have the second test of the competition. Enjoy your lunch, and the dessert will be on me. At 1:30pm everyone need to be ready in the living room waiting for Barbara wearing the outfit number 2. As for Grace, she sends her best wishes to everyone." Green light turned off, and Mister X gave his message with a sarcastic tone.

We all started talking at the same time. At least, we already knew that Grace was there with the competition organizer, and that Barbara probably came to get her before we woke up. But now are all worried about what would be the second challenge of the competition. Mister X spoke of dessert, would we be able to win a prize for some sweets? Or we will maybe have to eat as much candy as possible in the least amount of time to win the test? My thoughts were flying in my head until Daniel called me to help him holding the front door to the room, so he could bring more wood for the fireplace. So, I went to help Daniel, and we started a very nice conversation about our families, schools, hockey, and we even said that we missed our dogs. He was really nice; it was easy to feel good around him. Then John came over to help with the firewood, and we ended up sitting on the porch, and talking about the competition. Emily and Thomas as usual did not offer help or make the effort to socialize with us. It felt like we had formed a group outside, while Emily and Thomas had formed their group inside.

We all had lunch together, got ready and wearing that number 2 outfit that looked like a jumpsuit you use to paint the walls. We went to wait for Barbara in the living room. Again, punctually our instructor arrived. Emily questioned her: "Hi Barbara, what time did you take Grace, because none of us got to say goodbye to her?" and in response, Barbara said: "I can't discuss the rules of the game with you, so forget about Grace, and focus on the next test. Follow me please." Again, rudeness from this woman. It was difficult to understand why she acted that way, no one was there discussing it, it was just a question that we were all curious to know. Anyway, we arrived in front of this table, and saw several boxes covered with a black cloth. Barbara then spoke:

"Camila, as the winner of the last test I want you to choose a box on the table, and position yourself behind it. Then choose another participant, and say behind which box you want the person to be." I positioned myself and chose Daniel, and said I wanted him in the position of the box next to mine. Next it was Daniel who chose John. Then it was John's turn to choose Thomas, and place him in the box located at the end of the table. After Thomas was chosen, there was only one person, and one box left, so Barbara ordered Emily to take that place.

Once everyone was ready, Barbara asked us to remove the black cloths that covered the boxes and said: "I hope you guys have saved room for dessert. Inside these boxes you will find spices from the world cuisine, and you will have to eat, and count how many seconds you used to carry out the activity. Before speaking your time, you will have to open your mouth to show me that it is indeed empty. If you don't eat everything in there, you will be the loser of the test. The winner of the challenge will be the one, who says most closely in how many seconds he performed the task. The order will be the same with which you positioned yourself behind the boxes, and I will time it one by one. Now we start with you Camila. When I say start, you know, I have started the timer. My only suggestion to all of you is, be quick!

It was difficult to pay attention to Barbara, because I was terrified of seeing boxes of animal parts, and a glass of disgusting liquid in front of me. It all felt surreal. I thought about asking to be eliminated from the test before even trying, until I heard Daniel next to me whisper in my ear: "You can do it, Camila. Just swallow fast." It was then that I took courage, I held the glass that was inside the box in front of me, while I smelled that strong smell of blood I could read the label that said shake of fat with blood. I looked at Barbara nodding, and she started the timer.

I took the glass to my mouth while trying not to smell the blood that entered my nostril, I was swallowing sip by sip counting the seconds, until I quickly finished the glass. I looked at Barbara, opened my mouth and said: "6 seconds." The taste of blood in my mouth was horrible, the urge to vomit came and went, but I had managed it. It only remained to know if I had got it right in how long I had taken my shake. I looked to the side, and saw that Daniel was smiling, proud of my performance. And now it was his turn. In Daniel's box was a bowl of goat brains, and a note saying take one and enjoy. Barbara confirmed that he was ready, and started his test.

Besides, I just prayed that he would succeed and not be eliminated from this challenge. And Daniel did it! He took a brain and quickly bit it with the bill of his mouth and quickly chewed the rest. He ended his proof by saying 7 seconds. Now it was time for John to eat what was in his box. John had to eat an animal's eye, which he did remarkably without seeming to have any trouble. As soon as his test had started, he had already ended it, by saying: "5 seconds." Then it was Thomas's turn. In his box were live beetles. He quickly put a beetle in his mouth, made a movement with his jaw, and opened his mouth to scream, however, a piece of the beetle fell on the table and Barbara shouted: "You need to eat everything! Eat that piece that fell too." Following the instructions, Thomas ate the remainder, and opened his mouth to shout: "5 seconds." Finally, it was Emily's turn. In her box, there were live maggots, and she only needed to eat one. I've never seen a person complain, and make such a face while trying to swallow something. Her test seemed to be the easiest of all. Then Emily opened her mouth wide and shouted: "4 seconds."

It was then Barbara's turn to give the result of the challenge:

"Camila, Emily, and Daniel; the three of you are still in the competition. But between Thomas and John, we have the winner and loser of this challenge. One of you missed the time. The other one, who practically got his time right, passing by just 2 thousandths of a second on the stopwatch, and who will continue in this competition is you John. Congratulations, you go on, as Thomas shall bid farewell to you all."

I gave a shout of joy; I couldn't contain my happiness to know that my friend would continue with me in this competition. Barbara then said that we were all dismissed, and that we should go back to the house. As soon as I started walking I felt like I was going to throw up. I ran back to the house, and hurried to the bathroom. John followed me, and stayed there with me while I got over that nausea. I washed my face with ice water, and we returned to the room with the others.

Arriving there, Thomas angrily looked at John and said: "You're a shit, because you could see through the base of the box that there were beetles walking around alive, and decided to choose me, just to screw me. You are such a fool. Fag!" The atmosphere became tense in the room. Thomas approached John ready to hit him, and I pulled John to my side, while Daniel held Thomas to the other side. John didn't let it go either, threatening to go after him, and calling him a weakling. We managed to prevent the fight from getting heated, and Thomas went to his room, taking the opportunity to offend everyone on the way. We all stayed there, and took the opportunity to speak ill of Thomas's attitude, which was totally aggressive and unacceptable. We were fighting each other and losing control. Everyone looked haggard and tired. I think that, the idea I had of simply giving up, and leaving this competition had also crossed the minds of others as well.

It was time to take off those competition clothes that stank of animal corpses, and try to relax. No one was very well at that moment; everyone was somehow nauseous or retching.

Chapter 4
The Curse

I returned to the room feeling much better, without nausea or the urge to vomit, but I still felt that horrible smell of blood, it seemed that it had become impregnated in my nose. I saw that John was putting more wood in the fireplace, and I went there to sit next to him and asked: "Are you okay John? After the fight with Thomas, are you calmer now?" He looked at me with that ever-sweet look and said: "You know Camila, I got to the point where I try to ignore people when they offend me. When Thomas called me gay, he wasn't lying. I'm gay and I've had to take a lot of insults, especially where I come from, a very small town in the countryside."

I held John's hand, and told him I was sorry he had to suffer to be who he was. John continued: "Where I come from being gay is worse than a disease. Now things are calmer in my family, but when I told my mother that I didn't want to date the girl who lived down the street who had written me a declaration of love, because I was attracted to boys, she almost had a heart attack. They always say that mothers are more understanding than fathers, however, at home it was as if I had committed a barbaric crime, both my mother and father, could not look at my face. It took months before they were able to talk to me normally again, and still with some distance. We were never able to sit down, and talk about my homosexuality. It's a subject that they don't even want to know about, and I think that, because by not talking about it, they can end up forgetting, and managing to interact with the neighborhood, who all have such a big and sour tongue, that it doesn't fit inside their mouth. In a country town, everyone knows each other, everyone talks about everyone else, so my way of being, raised a lot of suspicion about my sexuality. Eventually, I got used to hearing comments behind my back, and insults at school, and I learned to ignore it. That's why Camila, relax, I'm calm." I was amazed at his posture, because I don't know if it was me I would be so polite. People at school are sometimes are very mean, not easy at all. I told John: "Look John, I just hope that when this competition is over we will remain friends, because I loved meeting you." Immediately John replied: "Of course, certainly Camila, and when we're out of here you need to visit my house in the countryside. In the city, there is not much to do, but at home we have horses, and they are super calm. There's a super cool waterfall too, and my dad set up a movie theater in the basement that you'll be impressed with. It's going to be cool; I promise."

We continued talking until Daniel joined us. Soon after Emily also appeared. We talked about the absurdity of the animal-eating trial, and how that experience made no sense to anyone. Emily commented that she wanted to leave, because she hadn't recovered from the test yet complaining of abdominal pains, and very strong nausea. Tears started running down her face as she spoke: "I just want to go back to my house; I can't stand it. I have never been so mistreated in my life. I wish I could talk to Barbara or this Mister X, and ask to leave in Thomas's place. Please guys, help me talk to someone, I need to get out of here. I am not well." Seeing Emily, that beautiful girl that I was initially jealous of, was heart-breaking. We were all very sorry for her, and called Thomas to talk. I tried to comfort Emily, but she wouldn't stop crying. Once Thomas arrived, we explained to him what was going on with Emily, and whether he would be okay with switching places with her in the competition, letting her go in his place.

Thomas said that was fine, that he agreed, but he raised the most important question: "How are we going to talk to Barbara or Mister X? We don't have any phone here, nor do we know how far they are from us, nor do we know how close they are." Emily, still crying, said: "And if we speak in front of the speakers? Is there no camera hidden in the boxes?" I still thought that, the idea of being monitored by hidden cameras was absurd, but it couldn't hurt to try. So, we spread out around the house in front of the cameras with signs saying: "Barbara or Mister X, we need to speak with you and is urgent." We waited for some sign of contact, and nothing happened. So, we tried to calm Emily down by saying that whatever the test was the next day we would help her, and that she could pretend that she was trying to do the test, and just lose so she could be eliminated. Still, she didn't want to be with us in the competition, much less with Mister X elsewhere. She said she was scared, and again that she just wanted to go home. I didn't judge her, because if it weren't for my friendship for John, and the feeling for

Daniel that was growing inside me, I would have asked to leave too."

We all agreed that that competition was unlike any other competition we had ever participated in, this one we were in now, didn't test our scientific knowledge or physical skills, it tested our resistance in the face of mistreatment, and fearful situations. It was hard to understand why they were doing this to us. What were they trying to test on us? We continued discussing what was going on, until Daniel made some observations: "Don't you find it interesting that we are all only children and just turned 18?" John said: "And my mother had difficulty getting pregnant, she went to a specialist."

Immediately, Emily, Thomas and Daniel confirmed that their mother was also unable to get pregnant, and only after looking for a specialist did they succeed. It was the same with my mother, and she always said that a specialist had done magic in her uterus, and placed a baby inside. I remembered what Ms. Smith said the week before, and I told everyone: "I know it may sound crazy, but could it be that our fathers and mothers didn't go looking for that indigenous entity, and made a pact to get pregnant? Last week in Ms. Smith class, I remember very well she telling the legend of the mothers who had the womb blessed by this indigenous spirit, and at the same time they received the gift of the womb being fertile to generate 1 child. Only they had to agree to raise the child with the right values, at least the values that the indigenous spirit thought was good. And then, according to legend, when they turned 18, these young people would be tested to see if they had learned the right values. Guys, do you think we are the cursed babies?"

Emily said: "I believe! Everything makes sense now." And Thomas added: "So if we are the children of the curse, Mister X must be the indigenous spirit?" Daniel continued the conversation: "In this case, Mister X, created this competition to test whether our parents taught us the values he wanted us to be taught. It has nothing to do with scholarship. This here is a trap. Do our parents have any idea where they sent us? Camila, what else does the legend say, because we also did a project at school on indigenous legends that manifested themselves in northern Virginia, but I don't remember anymore." It was my turn to try to remember everything Ms. Smith had explained. "Well, so according to the legend, parents know they need to let their children be tested, and they certainly know that this is the reason on why we are here. But I bet they couldn't imagine that, this indigenous spirit would put us in situations like the ones we've been through already. In addition, the legend was very clear when it said that if the parents did not let the child come to be tested by the indigenous spirit, they would suffer consequences that would affect their health. They had nothing to do, because the indigenous spirit, at the same time that he gave life to our mothers' wombs, he also threatened revenge." John said: "Is that why my parents got that way about my homosexuality? Does this indigenous spirit want to punish me? Guys, we need to get out of here!"

"Now I prefer to stay here, I'm more afraid to go near that Mister X, because he might punish me. What did he do with Grace? We need to get away from this place!" John squeezed my hand."

"But we can't leave Grace behind," said John. "And what is Barbara's role be in this story? Does she know what he's doing, and does nothing to stop it? What's up with her?," said Daniel. So, I said, I thought Barbara didn't seem to agree with this Mister X, because whenever I looked at her, she tried to smile at me. I think she felt sorry to see us there, but there was nothing she could do to stop it. Perhaps she had been cursed too.

We were all discussing how we could escape from there, after all we didn't know where we were, we didn't even have a phone or flashlight. We had no ways of getting out in the dark, in the middle of those woods, and we couldn't leave Grace behind. So, we decided that we would follow Barbara when she came to get Thomas, so we could see the way to rescue Grace, and then just find the way out of that place. John and Daniel volunteered to follow Barbara the next morning, while Emily and I would stand by if we received any guidance over the speaker. We finally had a plan to put an end to this absurd competition. At that moment, we had nothing left to do, but to try to rest a little. The day had been long.

Chapter 5
On the Other Side of the Mountain

That dawn was being difficult for the boys. John and Daniel tried to stay awake as long as possible, so they wouldn't miss the moment when Barbara come to pick up Thomas. Thomas in turn, had promised to make noise with his feet, so that the boys could wake up. The plan seemed to be working. Daniel heard Thomas's footsteps, and immediately alerted John. As soon as they heard the front door slam, they ran downstairs to finally find where is the other place. The place where they are taking the others participants. Very carefully, they went out on the porch, and saw that the van driven by Barbara was going up a mountain. It was still very dark, there was no lighting at all, but the boys managed to follow the car lights. They ran in the same direction that Barbara took Thomas arriving at the top of a mountain, and there they realized that the road only led to one more house. The dead-end street made everything easier. Even from far away, they were sure that was the house, as soon as they saw the car lights go out when it reached the end of the street. The walk from the old mansion to the other house was not difficult, it should have taken about 30 minutes, the only part that required effort was the climb that separated our house from the other. It was a very steep climb. Anyway, John and Daniel were excited as they now discovered the enemy's hideout. They also took a good look at the distance, and realized that the house appeared to be large, and had only one floor. They went back to the old mansion, and when they got there, they were so euphoric, that they didn't think about trying to sleep again.

The day began to lighten, and I heard the boys were downstairs talking. On impulse, I went downstairs in my pajamas without makeup, dying to hear if they've gotten any new information. As soon as I saw Daniel, I asked: "Tell me, did our plan work? Did you manage to find out where they are?" Daniel looked at me and smiled: "Yes Camila, and you will not believe this. We're very close. Now, we need to think of a strategy on how to get out of here. But first of course, we need to be sure which way the exit is." And Daniel was still looking at me with an adorable smile. I had to ask him: "And you seem to be really happy about that, right?" He looked me up and down, and replied: "Actually, Camila, I'm smiling at you. I had never seen you in pajamas, and without make-up. You were always all dressed up, even drinking the blood shake you didn't look disheveled. But I've never seen you as beautiful as you are now. Did you know that I think you're beautiful?" A red rose on my face, I was all embarrassed, and all I could do was say thank you. I wanted to say so many things at that moment to this boy, but I just stopped. So, I excused myself and went to catch my breath and change clothes.

After a few moments, the four of us were in the kitchen eating, and trying to think about how we would make our escape. We already knew where the others were, so we just need to find out if that road that continued in the opposite direction to the mountain would get us out of here. However, Emily reminded everyone of an important information. "I don't know if you guys remember, but when we were close to this house, the bus stopped for a few moments. What could be the reason for that?" John then said: "Maybe we are in a fenced area, and that stop was to open a gate or something." Then Daniel said: "Only if it's with a remote control, because I didn't hear anyone go down to open it." I got worried and commented: "I hope that if we're trapped inside a fenced area, at least we can get over the wall or gate, I don't know. The only thing that matter is to get out of here." Then Daniel said: "I'm going to finish eating, and then I'm going to walk in the other direction to see if I can see the exit, while there's still daylight. Does anyone wants to come with me?" Obviously I wasn't going to miss the opportunity, and said I would go with him, since John had left at dawn. Meanwhile, I suggested that Emily pay attention to the sound box, in case Mister X spoke about the next test of the competition.

We grabbed our coats, and Daniel and I headed towards the road. That day was nice even the sun came out and lit up our path. We started our walk towards the opposite direction of the mountain climb. Our idea was to see if that road would take us out of that place. It was a gentle descent with trees that practically formed a tunnel around us. We walked for a few minutes, and saw a relatively high iron gate in the distance that we would never be able to jump. It wasn't a common garage door, it looked more like an old gate that used a common key to open and close. The whole area was fenced off, so our only option was to get the key to that gate. We decided to go back, and tell John and Emily about our discovery.

As we returned to our old mansion, Daniel and I talked about our parents, and the apparent discomfort they felt in letting us leave the house to come to this mock competition. We felt sorry for them for feeling afraid of the curse of the indigenous entity. We also talked about how we wanted to leave that place, when he took my hand, and said:

"Camila, after this is all over, and we manage to get out of here, I want to keep seeing you always." Immediately I replied: "Sounds like a great plan to me." At this moment, Daniel stopped walking, took my other hand, stopped in front of me, and affectionately kissed me on the mouth. *How good it was to kiss him, that's all,* I thought. Not that I had experience, in fact, I had only given one other kiss on the lips in my entire life, but he was so affectionate that I felt in heaven. When he stopped kissing me, he hugged me tight, and said:

"We're going to get out of here, trust me. And I will take care of you." I simply smiled and said: "I trust you. I'm just afraid of what else might happen to us. I am very afraid of this Mister X." We made our way back, hand in hand. Within that nightmare that was living in the false competition, having met Daniel had been the best thing in the world.

Upon arriving at the house, we tell everyone about the gate. Really, our only possibility to get out of that place, was to get the key that was probably with Barbara or Mister

X. As no one had heard the bus stop for Barbara to get off to open the gate, Mister X should have the key. While we were discussing how to get the key, we were interrupted by the sound box announcement, it was Mister X: "Good morning participants! Today the test that you will participate in, will take place in the morning, in a little while, at 11am. I want everyone dressed in clothing number 3, and ready in the room waiting for Barbara, who will coordinate the fitting."

We all went upstairs, and put on the clothes indicated for the test, and to my surprise it was the diving suit. I got even more nervous imagining what test we were going to do. In a few minutes, we were all properly dressed, waiting for Barbara in the room. And as usual, she didn't delay, and asked us to join her. As soon as she finished speaking, I said: "Barbara, we wanted to talk to you, because we don't want to stay in this competition. We want to give up, and leave please." Soon after, Emily said: "Barbara, I'm not feeling well, I really need to go back home." Barbara looked at me, and replied: "Camila, I can't do anything to help you guys, the only person in charge here is Mister X, I just follow his orders, I'm sorry, but I can't help you. Come on guys, let's go to the test." For the first time, I saw that Barbara was a sweetheart with a good heart, she seemed to be as caught up in this competition, as we were. Hell, I was hoping she could help us.

We walked to a shed at the back of the house. We entered that place, and saw a kind of giant aquarium full of green and thin snakes inside it. My heart raced; I couldn't get into that. I saw that Emily was shaking, and I took her hand. Barbara, began to explain the test:

"You will all enter the swimming pool, and each one of you will have to go down to the bottom of the swimming pool to open a padlock. In the bunch of keys that each one will receive, you will see that there are 4 keys, but only 1 will open the lock. The winner will be the fastest. The loser will be the slowest. You can only leave the swimming pool, if you bring the padlock out." At the same time, Emily, in tears, said: "I'm not going to take the test. You can consider me the loser, I don't care. I will not enter this pool of snakes." Barbara with an air of regret replied: "You need to come in, Emily. As soon as I give the signal, the camera next to that speaker will flash the test to Mister X's monitor in real time. You have no idea what he can do to all of us, if you don't get in the pool. Please Emily, do this. As soon as I give the test start signal, I can't even talk to you anymore, because Mister X can hear. Don't get me in trouble." Now I was even more certain, that Barbara was just as much a victim as the rest of us, I just didn't understand why she hadn't run away. That couldn't be a job for her, especially after she said that Mister X was a guy we had to be afraid of.

Emily had no choice, but to participate. At that moment, we were all afraid. We all went to the stairs that took us to the swimming pool. Barbara asked us to get into the water, and position ourselves in our designated area. As soon as I entered, I felt the cold water penetrating the wetsuit. The water was so cold, that the clothes weren't enough, I even felt the air in my lungs go away. The snakes did not stop moving, and were constantly touching our bodies. So, we were all in the pool, with the bunch of 4 keys in hand. Barbara started the race. Daniel, John, Emily, and I were all in a panic. I took a breath, and went to the bottom of the pool, and tried to open my lock with one of the keys, but it didn't work. I changed the key, and tried again, and it didn't open. My breath was gone, and I had to go back to the surface. A snake had lain around my neck. I screamed when I pulled her out. I filled my lungs with air, and went back to the bottom of the pool, and this time I used the right key, managed to open my lock, and climbed up with it in hand. What a relief, I could get out of there. Reaching the surface, I noticed that John and Daniel were also returning with padlocks in hand. However, I noticed that Emily was moving underwater a lot. Looking back into the pool, I could see that Emily had dropped her set of keys at the bottom of the pool. Without going to the surface, she tried to make one more attempt by opening her lock, but things seemed to have gotten out of control. A snake wrapped itself around her arm, and when trying to get rid of the snake, she swallowed a lot of water losing her senses. I raised my head to the surface, and screamed: "Emily is drowning!" The 3 of us caught our breath, and went to the bottom of the pool to pull Emily up. Barbara was already on the ledge waiting to pull Emily's body out, when we caught up with her. Barbara quickly stretched Emily to the ground, and did the maneuvers to relieve the poor girl. Emily spat out the water she had drunk, and returned to her normal self. The atmosphere of tension had taken over the place, when we heard Mister X on the sound box announce.

"Today you Daniel were the big winner of the race, while Emily was eliminated for the day. Normally, the person eliminated leaves the old mansion only the next day, but given the circumstances, and Emily's discomfort, I want

Barbara to bring her here immediately. Have a great day."
We were outraged seeing Emily's fragility, and the coldness of that monster called mister X. More than ever, we wanted to get away from there. Barbara supported Emily, who still looked a little dizzy, and led her to the van while the rest of us walked back to the old mansion.

My mouth was purple from the cold. John, Daniel, and I couldn't even talk on the way back. The scene of Emily drowning doesn't get out of my head. Crying, I enter the old house, and was surprised by Daniel's embrace. He told me: "Just do one thing now: go upstairs and take a shower. Take off these cold clothes, because the three of us need to talk." I simply shook my head, as my mouth quivered, and did exactly as he said, threw myself under the shower, and let the hot water wash away the chill from my body.

Chapter 6
The Discovery

My body was already warm again, but my eyes were puffy from crying so much in the shower. The scene of Emily in the pool struggling to free herself from the snake, and then being rescued like a rag doll was just too surreal. I heard that the boys were also changing, and I decided to wait for them in the kitchen, while I prepared some hot tea to drink.

Everyone was scared with what had happened to Emily, and Barbara's words about Mister X been an evil. How evil could that person be? After all, he was just one person, he wouldn't have the ability to hurt us all.

Daniel arrived in the kitchen, hugging me, looking right into my eyes, and said: "I can see in your eyes that you are not well yet." I replied to him: "I can't forget the scene with Emily. She looked dead. I can't deal with this anymore. Please Daniel, help me get out of here." Daniel called John, and said: "I think we're all thinking the same here. We need to get out of here, because this feels like a trap to me, and I don't know how much worse it can get. We need to find that key that opens the gate. We can definitely go on foot. The problem is to be able to open the gate." John said: "You can count on me for anything. I even think that the 3 of us had to go to the house where they are, and break in with force, and break everything until we find the key." Daniel added: "So let's do this. Let's go this afternoon, and we'll have enough light to see everything. And Camila can stay here at the house waiting for us." At the same moment, I said: "I refuse to be alone, no way, I'll go with you guys."

In the blink of an eye, the three of us were walking towards another house. We were talking the entire time about where the key, that would open the gate could be at. It would certainly be easy to identify the key, because it was such a big and old gate, that the key must have be different from the ones we used today. But where would that blessed key be, was the question we asked ourselves. Maybe the key was in the kitchen, or maybe it was in Mister X's hands, or even, the key could be in Mister X's office. While we were considering all the hypotheses, we saw the house. By day, we could see that it was an imposing house, very well preserved, with only one floor and large windows.

John commented: "If we could talk to Thomas or Emily, or Grace too, that we're here to steal the key, they might be able to help us look around. It is easier for them since they are inside." I added: "Do they have any idea what is happening? Do they realize that this competition has nothing to do with competition, but rather an spiritual indigenous curse?"

Daniel said: "I think they know, because after Emily arrived at the house, she must have told them about the test where she drowned, and struggled to free herself from a snake. Besides, she must have said that we are trying to escape."

When we realized it, we were already very close to the house, so we were very careful not to get caught. We saw that the house had a main entrance, a side one, and then we saw an access that was also given through the back of the house. We were using the trees and plants, to try to stay hidden while approaching the windows. When we looked inside the first window, we saw a very spacious living room with a wall full of books, and some indigenous sculptures. We went ahead, and in the second window we saw what appeared to be Mister X's office, as there were several books and a table full of disorganized papers. I told the boys:

"We definitely need to get into this office, because it could be where the key is at. You can see there's a lot of things going on over that table." The guys agreed with me, and we moved on. We went to the next window, that had the curtain open, and we could see that it was a guest room. We walked on, and when we peeked into the next room we saw our friend Thomas sitting on the bed with a book in his hand. We made noise at the window and got his attention. When Thomas got up to come towards us, we noticed a horrible thing: he had the whole right side of his body paralyzed. He could no longer move like before. Not even his smile, and that competitive attitude weren't there anymore. "What a horror, what happened to him," was what I instinctively said, when I saw Thomas coming towards us with such difficulty. Thomas opened the glass that closed the window, and said: "Look what he did to me? He is an evil creature, and that story of the indigenous curse about pregnant women who sought his help is real. He was the one who performed the miracle, but now he is demanding it from us." We couldn't even react to his words, so Thomas continued: "As soon as I got here with Barbara, he took me to an altar, like a cave that is at the back of the house, and made this paralysis enter my body. I don't really know how to explain it, because I was a little dizzy, since he made me have tea before we went to that ritual place, but I know what he did to me was black magic, trust me."

I had no words to comfort Thomas, and I continued looking at him in perplexity, until Daniel intervened: "Thomas, hold on tight, because we're going to get you out of here. Have you seen Grace and Emily yet?" Thomas replied: "I saw Grace as soon as I have arrived, and you will not believe what that man did to her: she has no voice; the sound simply does not come out of her mouth when she speaks. And Emily, I saw that she entered the house this morning holding a respirator, and breathing with great difficulty." John said: "But what now? You are all cursed. We need to undo the curse first, and then escape." Thomas said: "That's why I'm reading, as well as Grace. We are looking in the black magic books that we found in the room for a solution that undoes the curse." We heard a noise approaching Thomas's door, and I quickly told him: "Stay calm, we're all going to get out of here. We will continue to search the house." Just before closing the glass window, Thomas said: "Look at the altar, try to find the grotto at the back of the house. It's hidden behind some bushes."

Daniel motioned for John and me to follow him. In a very low tone, Daniel said: "Now, besides the key, we need to find a way to undo the curse before taking them out of here. Let's go around the house carefully, to try find that mistic place." John and I nodded, and continued on to the next window, when we saw Emily lying on a bed holding a respirator. She looked so weakened, so fragile. I remembered her being pulled out of the pool, and now seeing her like that, tears ran down my face. At that moment, we had even more reasons to not be weak, now it was a matter of survival. We crouched among the plants, until we reached the other window. We were happy, because we had seen Grace alone in the room reading a book. We knocked on her window, and she came quickly to us. She spoke, but her voice just wouldn't come out. So, I said: "Hi Grace, I'm glad we found you. Don't worry, we're going to get you away from here. We already spoke with Thomas, and he said that you are looking in books about indigenous legends, some way to reverse the spell that the indigenous has put on you." I didn't even finish talking, Grace was already handing me a book, and went to get another book from table near her. With gestures, she showed me the pages she had marked, and I understood that I needed to read that. "I understand you, Grace, I got it. Let's take these books, and we'll learn a way to help reverse the curses placed on the three of you. We're going to the mistic place at the back of the house to see what's there. Stay well, and we'll see you soon, very soon." We carried the books that Grace had given us around the house.

When we reached the back of the house, we saw that there was actually a type of small church that was very rustic, resembling those caves that we see in rural areas, lined with river stones. As we approached that place, we went to peek through the windows to see what was inside. To our dismay, Thomas was actually right. That place looked like a black magic ritual mistic place, and we could see our pictures all there. Our photos were positioned there along with candles and incense. However, we saw that in addition to our photos, Barbara's photo was also there. We went very carefully towards the door, but it was closed. Daniel waved us out of there, and pointed in the direction behind some bushes. We all went there, until he said: "We need to get out of here, because I heard noise from the back door. If it's Mister X, we're done for it. I think we should go away, and stop to think of a plan." John and I nodded in agreement, and headed towards the road that would take us back to the old mansion.

As soon as we took some distance, I said: "Did you see that the picture of Barbara was also there? Could it be that Mister X also performed some spell on her? Maybe she wants to run away like everyone else." Daniel said: "I think there is such a chance, and that would be the best thing, because we could join it. No one better than Barbara to help us escape." I see Daniel grabbing my hand and smiling at me. "There must be a reason Mister X managed to hold Barbara here. So let's talk to her, and ask for her help," said John. We were so shocked by what we saw in that house, that we didn't even realize how fast we were walking. Time flew by, as did we our walk back to the old mansion.

The three of us were gathered in front of the fireplace trying to absorb everything we had seen. Initially, we only wanted to steal the key to the gate, but now that we saw our companions under the effect of the indigenous curse, we couldn't leave without undoing those spells. Well, Barbara was right when she told us that Mister X was dangerous. There was no doubt about it. The problem was how to undo the spells that were cast.

"Did Grace find an answer in the books? She made several marks that can help us find the solution. After all, she was there in the house, and had access to information that we didn't. Surely, the books will help us with something," I said, opened the book that Grace handed to us. Meanwhile, Daniel took the other book, and we dedicated ourselves to reading everything that had been marked there, in those pages of legends and curses.

We spent a lot of time poring over our readings and notes, as we shared our newest discoveries with each other. We weren't going to give up, even if we had to spend the rest of the day and night there, trying to reverse the curse.

Until John interrupted us: "Shouldn't we ask Barbara to join us? You remember her picture was also there at the altar, so she must also have some curse stuck on her body. I think we need to talk to her, and have her as our ally." Daniel added, "I think that if Barbara helps us we will succeed because apparently the Indian trusts her. I agree with you John, she needs to become our ally for us to overcome this curse." Then I said: "Let's do it tomorrow. After all, we have the penultimate test of the competition tomorrow, and she's coming here, so we could tell her that we saw our friends under the spell, and that we want to run away all together. And of course, ask her to help us." The boys agreed with me, and we continued talking about what we were discovering in the books Grace had given us. Until I found something interesting and said: "The mistic place is where the spell settles, and also where it disappears. Boys did you hear that? On that small church in the back of the house, is where Mister X makes the curses and puts the spells on people. His power must be associated with something on that place. Is there anything in your book Daniel, that talks about the altar?" Daniel replied: "Exactly about the altar, I haven't seen anything yet, but I saw a legend that said that black magic needs to happen in a place of invocation of spirit entities, and it only works if there is fire. Maybe there is a bonfire inside that mistic place, because we saw small sculptures that must then represent indigenous spirit entities, and our photos on the side." "Well, then that cave is the place where we will have to enter in order to undo the spells. So, we need to figure out how to do that. I'll keep looking in the book if there's anything else that can help us," I said. We stayed up late at night focusing in the readings, and at a certain point John said: "Guys, we need to stop for a while, and try to sleep, because we are exhausted, and we haven't eaten anything yet."

John was right, because our day had been quite long, we had seen Emily drown, we had found three friends under spells, and we still needed to find the formula that would undo the indigenous curse. My eyes were red from reading so much, in fact I was exhausted, it was time to try to sleep, so that tomorrow I would be in perfect shape to convince Barbara to be our ally. As much as we were figuring things out, time was against us, and I didn't want anything to happen to us, to any of us, not to me, not to my dear friend John, much less to that boy I had fallen in love with, Daniel. So, we did exactly what John recommended. We had a snack in the kitchen, while we exchanged the last ideas about what we had researched about legends and curses, and then we went to sleep.

Chapter 7
Competing in the Dark

We sat on the porch; it was a pleasant day, and we had to resume our conversation about the discoveries we had made the day before. Daniel commented on something that we hadn't mentioned until then: "Have you thought about what we are going to do with Mister X in order to be able to get away?" John replied: "If I have to hit him, I have no problem with that. I've been in so many fights that one more on my account, doesn't make the slightest difference." I said: "If I have to hit him, I will too. We just need to undo the spell, and then I don't care what happens to this man. But wouldn't we have to make a report to the police?" Daniel added: "The problem with calling the police is, that we would have to do it now, and not later when everything is resolved. Who will believe our curse spell story, nobody. Better forget the police." I couldn't resist, and let pessimism take over my thoughts, and I said: "But what if we can't get away from here? What if Mister X wants revenge? Could it be that the spells still continues working out of here?" We stayed there brooding over possibilities, and found that it was right to be smart and act on our own. After all, Mister X had already hurt our friends for no reason, just because they lost a test, so imagine if we gave him reasons to be angry. My god, I can't even imagine what he would be capable of doing. It was 11 am, and we were ready waiting for Barbara. As usual, punctually, Barbara appeared. As soon as she entered our house, I said: "Barbara, we know everything that is happening, because we went to the Mister X house yesterday, and saw our colleagues from the competition all under the effect of a spell. We even took some of Grace's books to try to figure out how to end the spells." Barbara replied: "Did you really go there? So now you understand, when I said that Mister X is dangerous."

I kept saying: "Yes, we even managed to spy on his altar with the images of black magic, but we couldn't get in, because the door was closed, but it was possible to see our photos including yours on his altar. We just want to free the others from black magic, and escape from here, we need you, please help us." Barbara then, for the first time, gave me a hug, and said: "I need you. I'm as bound as your friends are to a spell, and the only way we can end the indigenous curse is working together. But guys, now we need to do the test first, because if I take too long to show up at the test site with you, Mister X will be suspicious. Let's do the following: take the test as if we hadn't talked, and in the afternoon, while Mister X locks himself in his office, I'll come here, and l we can talk. Understand?" We all agreed nodding, and we followed her towards the test site. I saw that I already knew the place, it was the same shed where Emily drowned inside the aquarium full of snakes. I couldn't believe, that we were going to have to go through everything again. Until we entered the place, and saw that there was a narrow room with a closed door right in front of us. We stopped there, and at this point Barbara showed us a sign with a red light from the recording camera was right above our heads, so we got the message. We had to keep our mouth shut, because in seconds Mister X would see everything in real time, and now that we had Barbara as our ally, we couldn't lose everything.

Quickly the light turned green, and Barbara then started giving the test instructions. "Hello everyone, today is our penultimate day of the race, and as Mister X commented yesterday, today's race will have the presence of some new friends. Inside this totally dark and very narrow room, you will find a key that will open the exit door on the other side of the room. During this short journey, you may find some reptile friends, but they are not dangerous to you, but be careful when looking for the key, and I recommend not taking off your gloves until you find the key. The key will be on the ground or hanging from the ceiling just above your head. The test will be carried out one by one. Those who finish the test wait on the other side of the room. At the exit door as well as at the entrance door, there is a video camera that will record the individual time of each one of you, and the fastest will be the winner, and the slowest will be eliminated from the competition. Understand? We can start. Who will be the first?"

John extended his arm, and positioned himself until Barbara started the test. John then entered the dark corridor that was that place, and started looking for the key with the arms extended above his head. He kept walking, and felt that he kicked something on the floor, remembered to move more slowly. He went to the end of the room, and had not found the key, and needed to return. It was very dark, and there were things crawling on the floor, but he couldn't see what it was. So, he decided to walk on his knees, then with his hands he could look for the key on the ground. He followed, and touched what was the crawling being, and let out a scream that could be heard from outside. "There are alligators here! It's hard, I can't find the key." Barbara shouted: "You need to continue John; the key is right there." After a few minutes crawling on the floor, we heard John shout: "I found it!" What a relief, he was about to open the door and leave.

Then Barbara asked, "Who's next?" I said I would. I wanted to do that test right away, so I positioned myself at the door, and as soon as Barbara authorized the start of the test I started. I was on my knees on the floor, and I gently rubbed the floor with my hands, as if I were wiping the floor with a cloth. My hands felt the reptiles, but I was able to move forward despite the fear that made me shake all over. Until I suddenly felt the key. I gave a shout of joy, informing the others of my find, I quickly went to the end of the corridor to open the door. I took off my glove which made it easy for me to be extremely quick in opening the lock on the door. I achieved! I had passed that tunnel of horror, and was already on the other side with John. Now it was Daniel's turn. He started the test, and was doing something similar to what I had done with my hands, but with his feet. He was slowly sliding his feet on the floor, and let his arms be stretched out over his head. He was very fast. In moments, we heard him scream saying that he had found the key above his head, and ran to the exit door. It was a relief to see the three of us there together.

Barbara found us, and pointed to the speaker when we heard: "Congratulations Daniel, you won the race with great speed, and you are in the grand finale of the competition. It remains to be seen who will be by your side: John or Camila? Who made the best time between the two, and who will be in the final with you tomorrow will be Camila. Congratulations Camila, you used a good strategy during the race, and you will be in competition tomorrow while John, you were eliminated today. See you soon!" Mister X has spoken. Barbara instructed us to leave the place, and as we walked back to the house, she said: "I need to go now, but I'll come in the afternoon, so we can talk, but you can count on me already. We are going to end with Mister X game." Those words were music to my ears. We returned to our old mansion, still high on adrenaline, and sat in the kitchen to talk. "I can't believe we have Barbara as our ally, now I'm optimistic, and I know we're going to make it." I said with joy, "Camila, did you notice that she was also very happy to know that we want to end all this? I think she also needed us to destroy the indigenous curses, because before us, she was all alone against him," said John, and Daniel added: "I was just curious to know what her story is or why she is here, I didn't see any kind of spell on her. Why didn't she run away sooner?"

Chapter 8
The Ally

It was early afternoon when Barbara arrived. We were waiting anxiously and full of questions. As soon as she entered, we gathered in front of the fireplace, and I started asking why she was there, why didn't she seem to have a spell on her, why hadn't she run away yet? Then Barbara rudely interrupted me, and said: "Let me tell you the legend of the indigenous man that brought us all here, and then I'll tell my story, okay?" We all agreed, and made ourselves comfortable, because we knew there was a lot of story ahead of us. By the way that Barbara was behaving, what we read in the books that Grace gave us, did not represent anything close to what we would hear from her.

Then our new ally began to speak:

"Well, I don't know if you had enough time to get to know each other here at the house, but there are countless similarities that unite all of you participants. These are not coincidences, but part of the history of the legends of barren women who received the miracle of the indigenous man. All of you participants are children of couples where the woman was barren. Your parents sought out the indigenous man, who you actually know as Mister X, and asked him for the miracle of having a fertile belly just once. The indigenous man blessed your mother's belly, and they managed to get pregnant immediately, disregarding all medical predictions that did not believe that something so miraculous would be possible to happen. The indigenous man assured that the child would grow up healthy, but that when the kid turned 18, it would be tested. The indigenous man himself would summon the blessed children, testing the skills and values, that they had learned. He was going to see what kind of adults those kids had become."

I ended up interrupting, and asked: "But what's the purpose of the indigenous man testing children?" Then Barbara continued: "He wants to keep under his power examples of his own creation, those who were more warriors and represented the strength of the indigenous roots of his tribe. His tribe was named Botucu, was the most feared of the tribes, because it made curses using entities of nature. They were not always evil, but in order to survive the advances of modernity and civilization, the Botucu tribe ended up creating warriors equipped with many techniques to create spells and curses. So, the indigenous man wanted to find among you the best warriors and keep it here beside him. This faked competition has already happened twice before this one you are participating in, with a distance of 21 days between each. I participated in the last one, and was the winner, and because of that I was made a prisoner here." This time it was Daniel who interrupted: "But you couldn't run away? That day you came to pick us up, couldn't you just run out and ask for help?" Barbara continued: "It would be simple if the indigenous man had not cursed my family. It was by blackmailing me that he held me here. He said if

I ran away before it was my time, my family would pay. And you saw that he has the power for that, he can cast spells, so I got really scared, and that's why when you came to ask me for help, I said that I needed your help. Before my competition, there was the first championship, and the winner was Matthew. I know this, because I met him when I arrived here in my championship edition. Matthew was here, but he couldn't resist the things that he saw happening during my championship, and he fell into a deep depression that made him take his own life, just 3 days before you guys arrived. He hanged himself." John said: "How sinister that. The guy was so upset he couldn't move on. But what did they do with his body? And his parents?" Barbara went on to say: "Matthew's parents simply received the ashes of his body, that was cremated right here, after a ritual performed at that altar that Camila commented that you got to see. Obviously the parents knew that the Indian had done something evil, but the parents were totally without resources to fight against the indigenous man. What could they do? Nothing! It was the parents themselves who wanted to love a child so much, that in the past they agreed to put their child to the tested. So, you can imagine how I felt, after seeing the only person in that house that I trusted take his own life? We had already learned a lot about the legend and about the spells, especially Matthew, because he had been here much longer than me. But it was too much for him, he couldn't resist. At that moment, my world crumbled too. My hopes of getting out of here alive, were also gone. Above all, I felt completely alone. And alone, I wouldn't be able to fight him, but with all of you I believe we can beat him; we just need to know how to do it."

Barbara paused, while we looked at each other impressed with the story we had just heard.

Then she continued: "We need to stay together to neutralize Mister X. And from what I could understand by reading his books, all the spells that he does and undoes, happens in that mistic place behind the house, so we need to take Grace, Thomas and Emily to the altar with the Mister X inside there to undo the spells." So, I interrupted: "Yes, that was exactly what Grace had marked in the book that she gave us. She had read this ritual to undo the spell. All cursed people need to be in the same place where the spell was installed, and those small clay sculptures must be burned there, so that the spell burns together releasing the victim of sorcery." Daniel then said: "But how are we going to take the other three to the altar, and hold Mister X at the same time?" Then Barbara said: "I have a plan, and everything has to work, because we will only have one chance, so we cannot fail. Well, tomorrow I have to come here to get John, so that he can be taken to the altar, and receive the spell."

John intervened: "No, please, I don't want a spell placed on me. Let's end his life first." Barbara continued: "Calm down John. Listen to me carefully: every time the eliminated person arrives at the house, the Mister X prepares a portion, which looks like tea, and leaves the tea to rest it there for a few minutes in the kitchen. Tomorrow, as soon as the Mister X sends me to pick you up, he'll have the tea ready, so I'm going to throw his tea away, and replace it with some other common tea. Of course, without leaving any traces. And then, when the Mister X hands you my tea for you to drink, you take it and try to pretend that your movements are slower by deceiving him, that way the spell won't catch you. But it's very important that you pretend very well, and don't let him know that you didn't drink what you were supposed to drink. The tea he makes opens the body to receive black magic, and without the tea running through the body, the spell won't take hold. Once you've had all the tea, he'll make you hold the small clay sculpture that today is in front of your picture on the altar. At this moment, he will utter some words of black magic, and order that something in your body lose its function. This moment will be crucial John, because whatever he orders your body to do you will have to do, to deceive him." John said: "Pretend is something easy to me to do it, I've had to keep myself cool many times, I know I'll make it. But then what? How shall we do?" Barbara went on to tell her plan: "At this time that the fire of black magic will be lit is when we must look for the other three victims of the spell. So, what I thought was that Camila and I could use this time to run inside the house, and get the other three. You John will be there playing the bewitched, and Daniel will be ready for our arrival. Once we arrive, Daniel and John hold the old Mister X inside the altar, while Camila and I take everyone else inside, plus all the small sculptures and pictures. That way we'll be free of all spells, and we'll be able to get out. I believe the gate key must be in some drawer in his office, so when we go in to get the others, we can get it. The important thing is that they need to be very synchronized and you, John, need to fake very well to not unleash Mister X fury, even more." Daniel puts his hand on John's shoulder and smiles. "You can rest assured Barbara, because if you have someone who can keep a cool mind in a moment of stress is John, and we will make it." Daniel said: "As for holding Mister X, you can be calm too, John and I won't let him move until the spells leave everyone's body." Then Barbara ended by saying: "I need to go before the Indian realizes my absence. Now it's agreed: tomorrow I'll come for John when Mister X gives the order. Camila and Daniel can take a ride with me to a very close distance from the house, then Camila will be waiting for me at the front door and you, Daniel, go very carefully to the back of the house where the small church is, because that's where Mister X will be waiting for John. The rest we already know how to do. Now I need to go."

And that's how it was, Barbara left us in a rush. It took a while to process so much information. We sat there thinking about everything Barbara had told us. After everything she told us, I understood why initially she seemed so sad, of course, with Matthew's death she felt alone and helpless, on top of that being blackmailed by Mister X. I love my parents so much, that I don't even know what I would do if someone tried to harm them. Well, I'd probably do what Barbara did, put up with whatever it takes to make sure no one touches my family.

The silence was interrupted by John: "Tomorrow will be a great day for all of us. This competition set up by Mister X has its hours numbered." Daniel said: "Imagine the anxiety of Barbara who is there in the other house with the enemy, and will have a fundamental role tomorrow, by the way, just like you John. Thank you for taking a risk for all of us." John said: "That's it's man, we're together."

So, I decided to interrupt and said: "What do you guys think about having dinner earlier and try to rest, because we'll need to be 100% tomorrow. I don't even know if I can sleep, but a nice shower and a good dinner may help. Here's what I'm going to do: I'm going upstairs to take a shower, and then I'll make us a decent meal, okay?" Immediately I received a yes from the boys, I tried to get busy with my next tasks, and mainly try to relax my head that seemed to be boiling, because of the intensity of the last events. When I went down to the kitchen, I was already feeling a little lighter, and I did my best for dinner, I made a dish of pasta with Bolognese sauce just like my mother used to make at home. It was delicious! Everyone liked it, and took advantage of that moment of relaxation to joke about me hiding my cooking skills. Despite all the anxiety before the facts, and the day that was to come, being with Daniel and John was very good, both boys were incredible people. I wondered if it was, because they came from a spell or, because they were practically living miracles, but either way, they had become special to me, and being next to them was so welcoming, it felt so good, that for a moment I managed to forget why, because of what we were united.

I sat on the couch in front of the fireplace, while John put more wood on the fire. Then Daniel came subtly beside me, and sat very close to me. I let my head fall on his shoulder, and he snuggled me into his chest hugging and petting me. I felt like this was my newest favorite place in the world, in Daniel's arms. We enjoyed the fireplace, and managed to relax a little. John went upstairs to his room allowing Daniel and I to have some privacy. Then Daniel said: "Tomorrow if everything works out, we won't be here anymore. We'll be back to our normal lives," a big smile appeared on my face, "I can't wait for that to happen. What

Mister X put us through here, no one in the world should have to go through," I replied to Daniel, so he continued: "But I don't want to be away from you, I want to keep seeing you every day. If you want, we could date, so that I can always be with you." I ended up interrupting Daniel, and said: "I really want to date you Daniel." Without more words, Daniel lifted his hand to my neck gently, and we kissed, and hugged a lot. At that moment, I settled back into the arms of my now boyfriend, and enjoyed every minute there with him. We talked about everything, as if we had opened a new door inside of us, and shared all the thoughts that came to mind, until tiredness started to hit, and we ended up falling asleep right there on the old leather sofa in front of the fireplace.

Chapter 9
The Big Day

I woke up scared, not knowing where I was, until I realized that I was there, in the arms of the boy that on the first day of the competition I have laid eyes on him, and since then I haven't been able to take him away of my mind. I would like to stay there enjoying that moment, but definitely that wasn't the right day for that, we had a big day ahead of us. As I moved, I ended up waking Daniel as well. It was still dark outside, but we knew that Barbara would come early to pick us up, so we tried to hurry to get ready to assume our respective roles in the plan we had organized. The big day had arrived, and the anxiety had started to take over me, I couldn't even breathe straight from so much nervousness. After all, everything had to go well, probably that would be our only chance. I went up to my room to get ready, and collected my faith, putting myself on my knees on the floor asking God to protect John in his pretense scene in front of Mister X, and that we all had the courage to play our roles, and that our victory was blessed. In a few moments, Daniel, John, and I were ready downstairs having coffee, while we waited for Barbara. In the blink of an eye, Barbara arrived, and said: "Hi guys. Today is our big day. Let's all get in the van, and do everything as agreed yesterday. Daniel and Camila, you will go down a little earlier, and Camila will go to the front door and you, Daniel, will go to the back, and then hold Mister X inside the cave with John. In the meantime, Camila and I, we are going to get the other participants, and take them to the back too to remove the spell. And John, while drinking tea, pretend you are getting sluggish and kind of sleepy, like the energy is going out of your body. Do it slowly, so that we can save time inside the house to get the gate key from the office, okay?" We all agreed and moved on; it was time to put the plan into action.

Just before reaching the house, Barbara stopped the van, and quickly Daniel and I moved into our positions. Then Barbara followed along the side of the house, taking John on the way to meet Mister X, everything was going according to plan. As I waited for Barbara to come to the front door to open it, I felt the adrenaline rush through my body, the most alert I've ever been in my life. I heard the van stop, and the noises of the doors closing, I knew that was the time that John needed to pretend and deceive Mister X for our plan to work. Daniel was already there in the back, also watching John and Mister X movements. He could see Mister X reaching for the tea, which John calmly began to drink as Mister X kept talking about legends of indigenous warriors.

Meanwhile Barbara and I, we entered the house, and ran to get our friends. Barbara told me: "You go get everyone, and we'll meet at the office where I need to find the key to open the gate down the road." Without contradicting her words, I followed her plan. I got Grace out of bed, and quickly explained what was going on, while asking her to help get Emily, since I didn't know how weak she would be. Grace still a little dizzy, handed me a sheet of a book where she was showing the image of a knife with a handle all drawn with indigenous symbols. She still couldn't speak, so I quickly glanced at that sheet, and saw that the content said that to end the curse, the indigenous man needed to be killed with his tribe's knife, and be destroyed in the place where the spells were uttered. When I saw that information I was even more trembling than I already was, after all it would be a death, who among us would have the courage to kill another person. That wasn't part of our plans, much less still having to find the indigenous man knife. We just wanted to get back to our normal life, and escape from that place. From there, we looked for Emily, who was still breathing heavily, and then I called Thomas, who with great difficulty due to the paralysis on the right side of his body, walked with us to the office. Barbara was there opening the drawers, until I went over to her, and showed her what Grace had previously shown me. Thomas craned his neck, and agreed with what he saw, as if he had read it before. So, we continued searching Mister X office, until we found the gate key in the bottom drawer of his desk. Suddenly I heard Thomas: "Look here, right here on the shelf, it's the indigenous man knife. In the dagger appears indigenous draws, as well as in this book, and even has the name of their tribe, Botucu. I'll take the knife with me, because if it's like the legend says, we're going to need it."

We had what we needed, and we left through the front of the house, walking around it, until we reached the cave where we could see Daniel. We could hear that, there was a different type of music playing, it seemed like a type of percussion, only instruments, and we could see that John was moving very slowly, as he entered the cave. Mister X made him stop inside a circle on the ground, while the fire on the side was burning very brightly.

At the same moment, Daniel positioned himself right behind the cave door, so that when the Indian took the small sculpture that was next to John's photo, Daniel entered the cave, and together with John they dominated Mister X holding his arms. Mister X couldn't believe what he was witnessing, while Daniel shouted giving the order for us to get in there too. We were quickly inside, taking all the photos, and small sculptures that we saw on the altar, and positioned ourselves around the bonfire, as the legend said it had to be done. We threw the images and sculptures into the fire, and they weren't just ours, there were other faces that we hadn't seen before, but they seemed to be other victims from the past competition, so we tried to get absolutely everything. We threw all those symbols into the fire, and we could witness the spells leaving the bodies, one by one.

First, we could hear Grace's voice return to her speech, then Thomas's body movements returned to normal, and finally we could see Emily smile relieved breathing normally again. However, the bonfire was burning intensely, and figures of indigenous spirits began to appear in the air, rising above our heads while Mister X shouted: "You will pay me! You are insulting the spirits of my tribe." As he screamed, the spirits swirled above our heads, as if they were going to attack us. Daniel and John were still holding on to Mister X, until he managed to break free from John, and picked up a dagger to stab Daniel. But Daniel only had time to take a step back before Mister X tried to attack him, but he missed. However Barbara didn't miss the opportunity. She had taken Thomas's knife and, gathering all her rage, she took the strength and stabbed Mister X right in the middle of his belly. The knife went in so deep, that all we could see was the dagger throughout his back. Mister X felt to the ground, as the figures wheeled, and screamed above the fire. Daniel pulled me by the arm, and said: "Let's get out of here now, quickly."

We ran out of the cave, but before entering the van, we managed to close the cave from the outside, leaving the still alive body of Mister X inside next to the fire. We all got into the van and Barbara, still shaking with blood on her hands, took us towards the exit. Upon arriving at the gate, Grace and Thomas got out of the van, and very skillfully opened the large gate that kept us hostage to our reality. We were all together inside the van, without any spells cursing our bodies, and we were finally free to go to our homes. I couldn't contain my tears, as I held Daniel's hand, I just thought that we had overcome all the evil that had been destined for our families. We were winners. I looked at the face full of tears of each one of my new friends, and I could see what Mister X was looking for: a warrior. Inside of each one of us, there was indeed a warrior, each one with their skills, competences and also defects, but above all, we had the values that made us fight for what was right. Then I looked back, I saw the cave burning in flames, the flames also taking over the sky. I was so focused on the flames in the sky, that I didn't even notice a vast distance growing between us and the cave, I heard Daniel whisper in my ear: "This is all going to die here, in the past. Ended! The only thing that will continue is the two of us, this has only just begun."